MONISHA K GUMBER

DOLLY WON'T PLAY

A story in free verse...or whatever

It was the best of times, it was the worst of times- From a Charles Dickens' novel, A Tale of Two Cities

Starry Starry Night- by American singer and song writer Don McLean in a song about Vincent Van Gogh

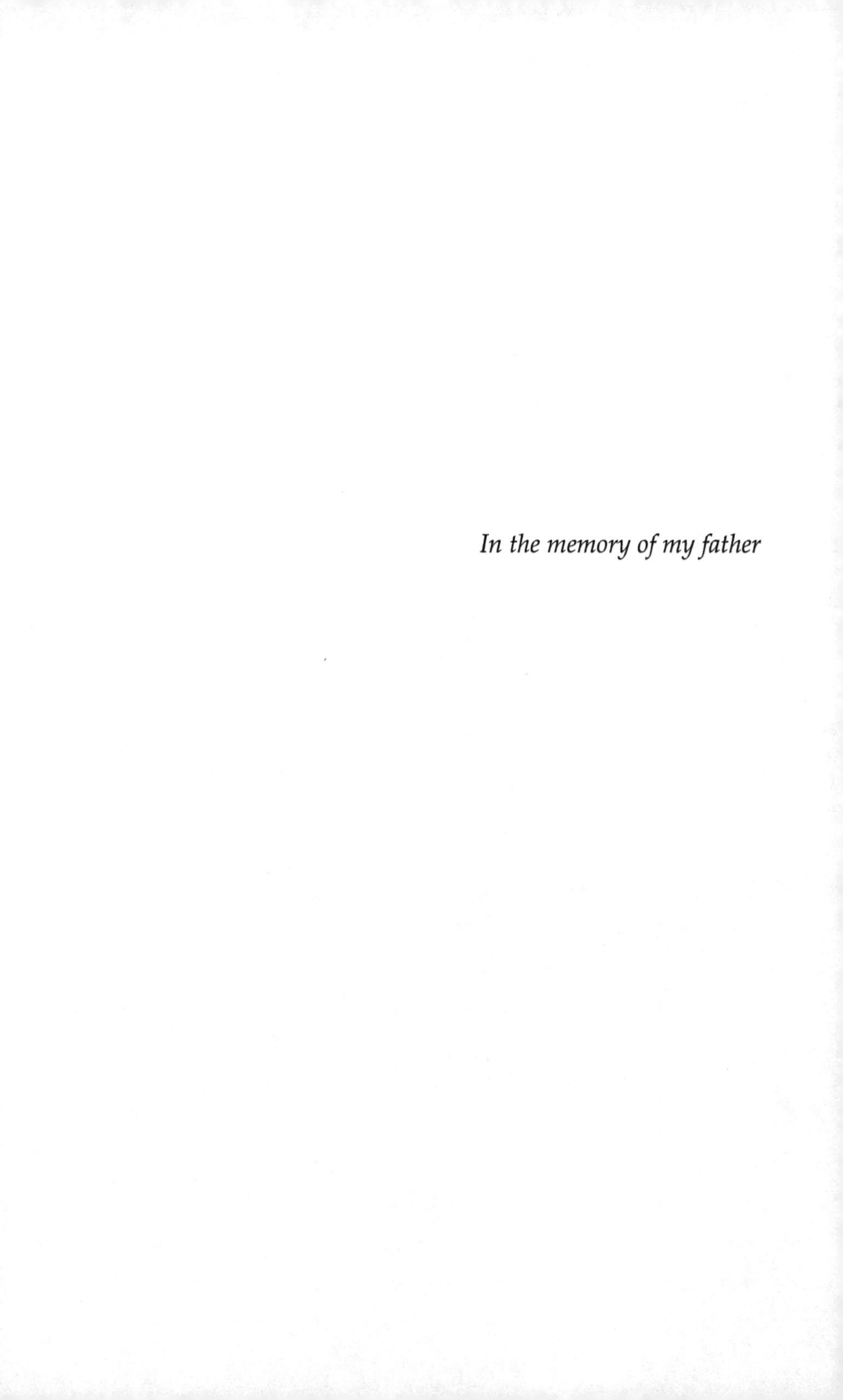

In the memory of my father

Goli maar bheje main, bheja shor karta hai

—from the movie *Satya*

Part I

Growing-up Pains

DOLLY WON'T PLAY

How do I start

that it sounds oh-so-smart?

Or should I just concentrate on being me?

—just a pretty face

and a superb figure

Welcome to my world

of make-up, false eyelashes, push-up bras and
report cards

with lots of red lines

Yes. The Dumbo is going to write a book.

Have no expectations

have

nothing to lose

except if you paid to read the book

which I doubt . . .

It's a bright, bright, bright

sunshine day . . .

blue sky above and lush green grass

on which I lay.

Wet kisses on my cheeks

being hugged so tight

somehow it doesn't feel so right.

Uncle is so nice and warm

and frankly,

hasn't done enough to raise an alarm . . .

So my feelings

I learn to fight

even though

it still doesn't feel so right . . .

I see this stunning woman

my mama

walking towards us

Uncle gives her a hug, too

A hug

that should have ended

a minute sooner.

I feel a pang of

jealousy . . .

Towards whom?

They say they are friends,

best friends

But *ladka ladki kabhi dost nahi hote*

Nani and I again watched *Maine Pyar Kiya* on TV
the other day

But they're grown ups

Man and woman

Is Uncle my mother's friend?

Or mine?

Papa and Mama

fight a lot,

all love is lost

You see, Papa, a smart doctor

Mama, an ex-Miss Delhi

Smart and dumb

don't go together

You are the biggest

mistake of my life

Papa lashes out at her

Mama rolls her eyes

because this beauty queen

doesn't have the words

that can hurt

My brother and I

two dumb-bells

taken after our mom

so says Papa

Bhaiya gets beaten up a lot

but not me

I am just a cute little girl

A *kanjak*

Dolly, you are so sweet

like an ice-cream . . .

You know it, don't you?

I could eat you up

He licks his lips

the lift door opens

I run off

but a part
remains

with my
uncle

School starts

Time to get serious

We are big children now

in Class 4, no less!

Come-onnnnnnnn-childrennnnn-dictation-time!

A lullaby

yet my heart beats louder

then fades away . . .

I hear the cruel words

bounce on my empty notebook

Ma'am pulls it away mercilessly

as I try to hold on to it desperately

She looks at me contemptuously

as if I am a criminal

even though she just robbed me

of my self-respect, my notebook

Come-onnnnnnnn-childrennnnn-dictation-time!

Home wasn't so happy, either

but I loved them all

especially my dad

He was too good

for the rest of us

or that's how

he made us feel.

I ached for his affection

a hug here, a kiss there

None came . . .

Except a shrug of his shoulders

like

Where did I go wrong?

But Uncle filled in for Dad

and gave me

more than I could ever ask for

My handsome Uncle Uday, my hero

Come on, Dolly

let's go high

He pressed

the button of the lift,

we elevated

before he put me down

to play

on the bed

And made me take a God's promise

never to tell a soul

and if I broke it

my mom would die,

the devil would kill her

It was all part of God's mission

A part of me knew

he was making it up,

a part of me believed him

because a part of me wanted

what he wanted

Love

So that Mom could live

forever

That's what I told

myself

Did it hurt?

Or

did it feel nice?

Or both?

After so many years

I still feel ashamed to say

Yes. It did

Sex is not overrated,

it hurts like hell

it feels good

it is supposed to

Both

Can I describe it?

No, I am not good with words

and I don't want to

What Uncle and I had

was too personal

sacred

an act of being loved

finally

But I did it for Mama.

You know that, don't you?

School again.

I jump

from one place to another

One topic to another

School

They called my parents

to say I needed to be

evaluated

professionally

What was that?

They said I was slow. Lost. In zombie land.

It's not just academics

she mutters to herself . . .

she just doesn't respond . . .

and stares away into space

My dad refused

to believe

I was his daughter, after all

Mom did

I was her daughter, after all

Colourful educational toys

jig-saw puzzles, stacking cups, Mr Potato head

some broken crayons

No sweat

Except this doctor

asked me

my favourite colours

my friends

my hobbies and

what did I want to do in life

Yes, grown-ups are crazy

even the well-meaning ones

From the corner of my eye

I see my mom

wiping her tears, her eyes looking elsewhere

I know

she knows

ADHD

Attention Deficit Hyperactivity Disorder

But Dolly is, you know . . . Mama said

kind of lazy

a daydreamer

she isn't hyperactive

Well, the doctor says

there are all kinds

all variations

and depends on the degree of the problem.

But that was me

that was God's way of punishing me

for playing with my uncle

and enjoying it too

instead of praying

for my mother's life

that I

screwed up

Big time

Don't cry, Mama

I will never do it again

Do what, Dolly?

Mom's eyes pierced into mine

I mean, I will learn my spellings

Oh, Dolly!

What will I say

to your father?

That was her biggest worry

I will sue her

she doesn't know a thing

Dolly is my daughter

she can't be

what I can't be

My father

still

hoped

that I could not go wrong

but I did

I had a disability,

a learning disability, as they say

which meant I wasn't normal

I wonder

who is . . .

My friends

Tara and Megha

Tara—funny yet rebellious

Megha—always a winner

read books I dreaded

Bizarre names like *Matilda, Of Mice and Men,
The Wind in the Willows* . . .

What if they found out

that I was different?

So I focus

on a story

Megha is narrating

A movie based on Ruskin Bond's novel

'So, you see, Khatri's life becomes miserable as everyone boycotts him in the village. Biniya is a kind girl who sympathises with Khatri and decides that Khatri is the real owner of umbrella, not her. She gives the umbrella to Khatri. The village people accept him, then . . . and then . . . Guys, that's about it . . .'

concludes Megha proudly. As if it was 'her' film.

I can't take it any more

I go home

Dolly, come on in . . .

Uncle holds my hand

gives me a gift

a Barbie doll

My fingers stroke her silky hair

touch her full chest

wrap around her slender waist

feel her long legs

and drop her hard on the floor

who could be envious of a plastic toy?

But what if Uncle notices the stark differences, too,

and stops playing with me?

But Uncle smiles

reassuring me

and I melt

to the taste of refreshing peppermint

So, where have you been?

Wasting time with Megha and Tara?

Papa shouts at me

'So, you see, Khatri's life becomes miserable as everyone boycotts him in the village. Biniya is a kind girl who sympathises with Khatri and decides that Khatri is the real owner of umbrella, not her. She gives the umbrella to Khatri. The village people accept him then . . . and then . . . Guys, that's about it . . .'

I conclude proudly. As if it was 'my' film

Papa's eyes

burning balls of red fire

Phataaaaaaakkkkk!!

I collapse

And this time

I really did zone out

Sorry, it was a blackout

My head still spinning and

an extreme pain

deep inside me

It was the middle of the night and my body seemed
to be on fire.

Mama . . . Mama . . . I called out

Shhhh . . . baby, I am right here
And found my mama next to me
Mama, did you see that? Papa hit me…
I cried while my little body shook
probably to shake off the
betrayal

I remembered those times

when he took me out on drives for ice-cream

when I was still at nursery school

I guess back then it didn't really matter so much if
you couldn't spell 'slide'

as long as you knew how to play on it

'Dolly, I am with you, always . . . no matter
what happens'

We hugged each other to sleep

Thankfully it was a weekend and

despite the filmy slap,

which hurt, by the way,

I was happy

that I didn't have to go to school the next day

School

A place having a loving and supportive atmosphere
where children develop emotionally and academically
where children reach their full potential
a nurturing environment that develops confidence
We all know it's nothing but
propaganda

In reality, for kids like me who felt out of place

who couldn't focus in class,

who were sniggered at,

avoided by most children

it was a nightmare

I was bullied

Everywhere

By the teachers

the nastiest of bullies

at least some of them

Every time I got humiliated by my teachers

I felt tears trickling down my chapped red hot cheeks

More so because I couldn't bear their proud smiles
(my friends')

that they were trying hard to suppress

Children can be cruel

How I wish parents would teach them

the true meaning of kindness right from the beginning,

which is, being nice

to the weak kids in class

and the fat ones, the short ones, the weaklings, the *dheeley*
screws, and all the other kids who don't

fit in

I know you have heard this before

so nothing I will say will do anything more

In other words, school sucked.

I hated every minute of it

sick of those never-ending tests,

the attitude my friends were developing and

that

there was nothing I was good at

Yes, no singing. No dancing. No sports. Nothing at
Annual Day functions.

Not even a hint of extra-curriculars

It was *that* bad

At age nine, I was already destined to be

A F A I L U R E

in life

Meanwhile,

my personal life rocked

more and more

Oh Dolly, it is the best gift you can give to your
Uncle Uday

You are so beautiful, Dolly . . . so soft . . . red cheeks

I can never have enough

of you . . .

My body jerked in response

It felt good

Electrifying

The feeling of letting go and drowning in muck

it liberated me and

I was hooked

I was dirty

Finally

It felt refreshing to admit it in my mind

Uncle knew it, and still accepted me

despite my problems

despite my grades

despite what my teachers thought of me

despite being hated by my dad

He loved me. And that was all I cared for . . .

But remember, never to tell anyone

I promised Uncle

I meant it, you see

For once,

I wanted

to make an elder proud of me

The boat rocked

in the storm

I couldn't

hold on

with a moan . . .

went down

deeper and deeper

in the whirlpool

of my pee

Do you know you could replace the word 'Whirlpool' with 'Suckhole'?

Funny, no?

And so apt for my situation

Oh no, Dolly . . . you did it again.

Mama swallowed a lump in her throat

as she opened the drapes

to let the yellow

light

into the dark room

but the prison

inside me

remained black

You need to get out, Dolly

from your bubble

We have work to do

said my mother

to herself

A dumb beauty

took to Google

and read and read and read

until

she had enough words

to talk about it

Dolly isn't doomed, neither is she mentally retarded

Ok, she can be impulsive, or have problems with communicating and relating to the world around her and has a hard time concentrating

but a lot of kids like her are super intelligent and super talented

If it makes you feel better, then

do you know what little Dolly has in common with these famous people

Justin Timberlake, Michael Phelps, Sir Richard Branson and countless others?

ADHD

said the doctor

No, it doesn't make me feel better

because we don't know even one famous person from our country of a billion-plus people who has this.

But they do, Mrs Nanda

they just don't talk about it.

And that's why

Doctor

I am sad . . . Mama said softly.

So, you see, Mrs Nanda, I knew there was a problem

Aren't you glad you took Dolly to be evaluated
professionally?

said my class teacher, seeming more cheerful than ever

as if she had won a free comb with hair oil.

Kindly look for

a special school

for such children . . .

She can't stay here

Finally. Some sympathy.

All Dolly needs is some support

my mama replied

Like some personal attention in class, some extra time to do her work

some sensitivity

Today it's Dolly

tomorrow it could be your kids

whatever age they may be

Today it's ADHD, tomorrow it could be autism

Times they are a-changin'

adding more and more stress

taking a heavy toll on the kids

Surely as a teacher,

you can see that, can't you?

And have you not seen

Taare Zameen Par?

My mother roared

as if a movie should now

provide credibility

to her claims

of her daughter

wired differently

Oh, I underestimated you

but I see your point

Let's meet in a few days

and discuss

My teacher surrendered.

So Mom had tamed this bully

And that's why they say that

a mother's love

is the most potent force in the world.

I wonder why they consider me dumb

even when

I use such smart phrases

So my mother became

the first therapist

I ever had

Just like your mother

was to you

She asked me to look for

words in a game of

word search,

just five

A daunting task

But she pushed and pushed

and didn't let me give up

I ended up finding more,

even words which

weren't there

in the first place

and even the words I hated.

As I said, mother's love . . .

that starts much before they

push and push

in the maternity room

Girls just have it in them

despite the pain,

too much love to give

sometimes . . .to the wrong people . . . knowingly.

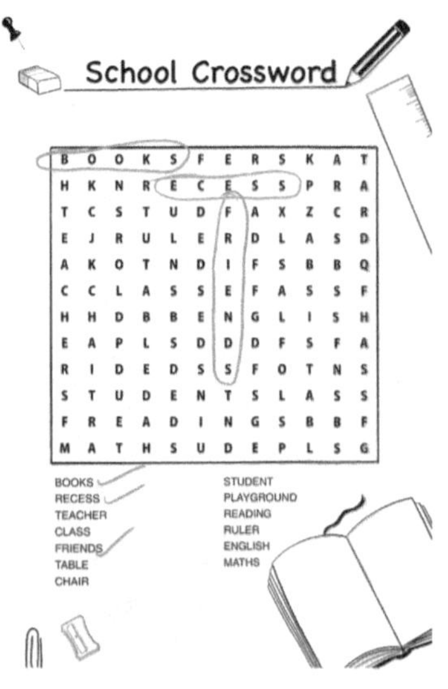

We bonded over

words and words and words

She taught me so many

some of them really impressive

only I don't know

if I always use them correctly

Learning disabilities or not

I could learn now

Ok, at my own pace

in my own way

All children are different

they talk different

play different

look different

learn different

Everyone knows

Then why the labels?

Why brand us for life?

Does it make it any better?

What's the rush to *fix* us?

What's the hidden agenda?

But then . . .

I was too young

and Mama too overstrung

with no respite from the frustration

of having no answers to these unasked questions

Henceforth (wow, I like the ring of this word)

we did

what we had to

and sure enough

I started doing better

and better

I wanted to stand first in class

I studied and studied

But it just didn't happen

Henceforth (wow, I like the ring of this word)

I asked my mother

is it impossible

because of the way I am?

Dolly, nothing, nothing can come in your way

just keep trying

Once I knew that

I gave up

trying

Milky white

hair as black as night

big eyes

that, too, light

Already

little girls were mean to me

I didn't want more hate

than my nine years could take

I settled for 'dumb beauty'

even when I had ideas

and theories

and concepts

and what not,

only I could not

express them properly

So I tried to remain deaf

to being called dumb

but couldn't get used to

the shit

especially because the shit was true

Instead of a simple cotton suit

Mama wore

black stilettos

and a skirt

with a red silk top

to a school meeting

and asked them to see

beyond their invisible glasses of racism

that size up, judge and compartmentalise

people

as smart, intelligent, genius, crazy, stupid, slow, gone case,
high class, low class . . .

based on the brands

they wear

on their bodies

or actually

how they speak

words

of the English language

in Hindustan

Mama became a warrior

she fought my case

at school

at home

defended me

believed in me

She didn't care what the doctors said

or what the internet said

Maybe

it would have been easier

if she could admit

that God made me this way

She KNEW I would overcome it

that there was no need for repentance

and it wasn't a life sentence

But my life ended

when Uncle Uday left the city

for greener pastures

or pinker little girls

Armies of hundreds of them

invaded my mind

I surrendered to them as

I couldn't let go of him.

But his body went

without goodbyes

except a call to his best friend

Mama

She felt even more defeated

than I did

What did this man do to his

women?

I just ran away—got on to a rocking horse

in the nearby park

I rocked and rocked

and rocked some more

rubbing myself violently against the saddle

as my poor mama stood watching

with her eyes blinded

drenched in hot tears

It felt good and I continued rocking

to get the same feeling

Uncle gave me

The rocking horse failed me and

I collapsed

on the beast.

Incomplete.

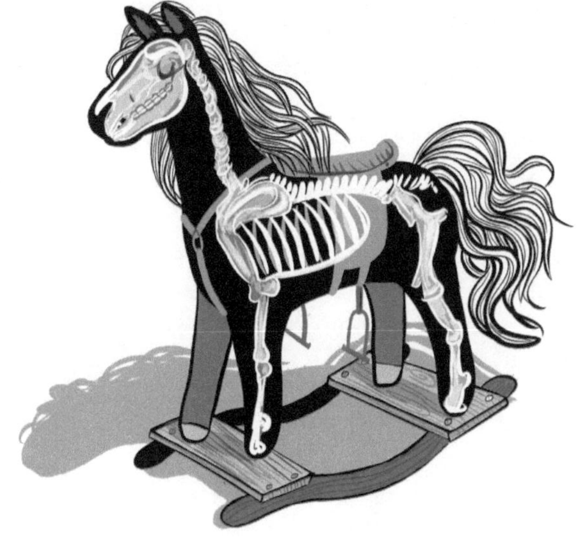

Now her trembling body

drenched in cold sweat

she became super-desperate

despite her belief in me

she started believing

in everything else too

occult-shocult, tantra-mantra,

energy healing, *pir baba* . . .

Maybe something would work?

So that her Dolly could

be like

other girls

Papa stood his ground

wouldn't let her try

anything on me

She promised

And the very next day

took me

to that place

I whimpered

I saw myself descending a black hole slide in the water
park,

a black hole that had no light at the end of it

or maybe no end at all

Look at me! the old woman in a black robe yelled

and shook my shoulders

Let go of me, Aunty . . .

I won't trouble anyone again . . . I howled.

Yes, I knew you were in there

leave her body

out, you witch! and she smacked me with a broom

to chase away the evil spirits

The mother spirit, however,

awakened

in Mama

and she knew

it was a mistake

She rescued me from the dusty dark alley

and promised

to herself

to protect me

from everything evil

A promise made

too late

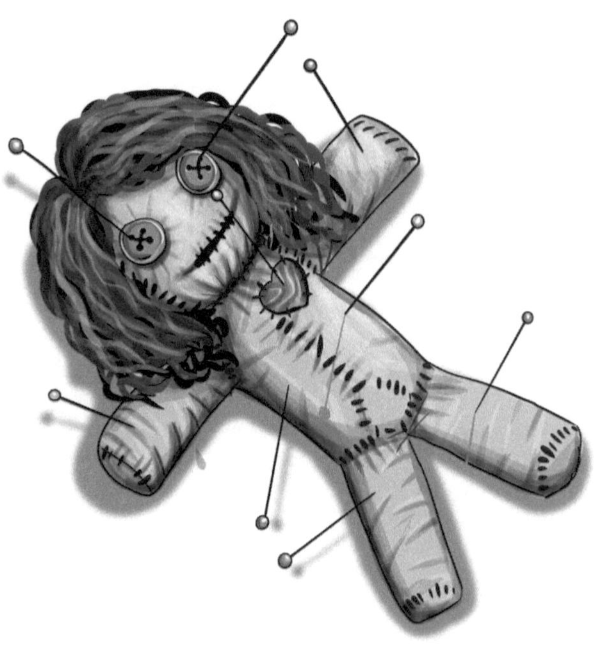

Dejected

heart-broken

confused

Lonely. Very.

Our games in bed had

cast a spell

The intensity of self-contempt combined with

fierce yearning

for the potion of love

rendered me helpless

an addict

on the brink of insanity

But life goes on . . .

We somehow managed

to pass each year

in school

The tag of 'dumb beauty' stayed

even when I could focus

a lot more

on words and numbers

written

on the blackboard,

much like the stories held as hostages

scripted

in my head

struggling to break out

till

I stopped peeing in bed

and

became a teenager

And

65

Fell in love

with Uncle Uday again

Nearly

Part II

Love is in the Air . . .

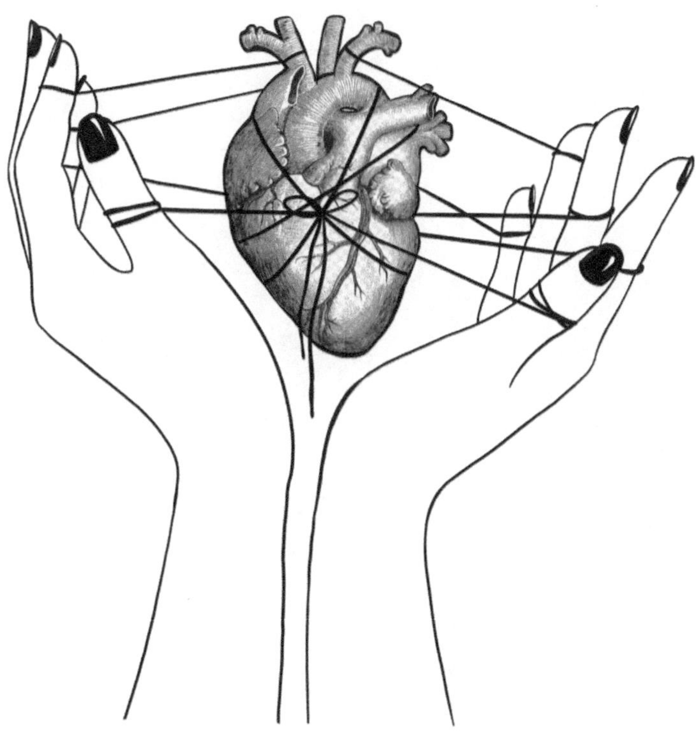

I know it's the wrong time

to introduce the characters

of this story

but I never did

anything right anyway

Tara, Megha, Karan, Mama, Uncle Uday . . .

Sandy, my brother, too

who hardly has a role to play here—

fragments from my twisted mind

from books

written earlier

We all were neighbours

lived too close

for our own good

Is this introduction enough?

Then let's carry on . . .

and take a time leap

just like they do in TV serials

I was now

a really, really pretty teen

like Betty and Veronica from Archie comics.

Somehow

girls wanted to hang out

with me

and show me off to other girls

to evoke jealousies

Why does no one tell them

it's wrong?

Even when I felt vindicated

that now it's my time

as no matter what,

these girls

could never

have half my figure

Even if it was wrong

I didn't want to change it

A recluse like me
welcomed the attention
It was long due
and I deserved it

Tara, my best friend,

was in love

with this guy

I had not paid any attention to

but when I saw him

looking at me

I fluttered my eyelashes

and welcomed him

in my space

even when

I knew

how my best friend felt

even when

she told no one

but all knew

It was Karan

Uday Uncle's son

Until now I did not really notice

but when he looked at me

with the same brown eyes

my body shivered

and reminded me

of his maker

Someone

I didn't even try or want

to forget

and move on from.

The contrition

(you can look it up, just in case)

mixed with recollections

of being in a trance

away from the realities

of the other world

was now my identity

and I craved for it

His voice

a softer version of Uncle's

with the same tone,

his hands

a shade darker,

his hair

thick

unlike Uncle's

But he was the best replica

of my lost love

as his mouth

was exactly his

father's,

brought back the memories

that had never really left me

and it was enough

for the time being

till Uncle came back

and reclaimed me

Well . . . I am in college

Dad lives far-far away

in foreign lands

That's what Karan told me

when I asked him

You go to which school and

what does your father do?

(*besides drive me crazy*)

Little did he know

that his dad has lived in my room

since I was a little girl

What was I to do,

except

settle for his shadow?

At fourteen, the hormones raging in me

were making it impossible

for me

to sleep

without reliving

the moments

from five years back

when I was just a little girl

and now

with my own

chest

rounder than Barbie's

and legs

longer

than hers

Oh that would please Uncle so, so much

I didn't have to do much

just pouted my lips

stroked my hair

acted a bit more

dumb

than I was

to get his attention

I know I hurt my best friend

but

I had to

get him at all costs . . .

but as I said

he came cheap

Young love

so innocent

he sent me

a million messages on Snapchat

cute animal videos

some memes

borrowed from the internet

love poems

that rhymed

funny selfies, too

with a filter that made him look

so much like Uncle

but so unlike him

Uncle had

what his son can never:

the power to possess

Whereas Karan, poor young lad,

even in college

wasn't man enough

to admit

he wanted me

or perhaps he didn't

and he really was innocent —

something that had begun to bore me

as this school girl really wanted to see

who was better

hoping that Uncle was . . .

so I could have no excuse

to get over him

I was desperate,

wasn't used to

this claustrophobia

of public places:

meetings at Comic-Cons,

the society park

or PVRs

If it was love

Karan had to prove it

but I was the girl here

and didn't want to

be too available,

which I was

but exclusive

to his bloodline, though

Yeah,

I am not a bimbo

I said to myself

School

as usual

boring

tiring

irritating

etc., etc.

but I had to still go

since I was just a young teen

and was expected to spend half the day there

even if I spent it daydreaming

in dusty classrooms

reverberating with giggling sounds

stench of half-opened tiffins

passed around during algebra lessons

interrupted by

a loud *Class! Be quiet!*

or in the girl's toilet

spending hours

adjusting my skirt

my hair

my bosom (because it's still school. Ok, boobs.)

applying layers of make-up

to get the

no make-up look

to attract boys

I had

no interest in

And, of course,

you already know

I claim no potential

in Math and Science

or English

though I have come a long way

can focus a lot more

can write a 300-word essay

with commas, apostrophes and capital letters

in the right places

unlike here

where I have the freedom

to write

without any fear of Cs or Ds.

A notebook

confined, limited, chained my thoughts

. . . but this laptop

Where my words are not forbidden

has no judgement from God

or the random Adam or Eve

who would

ultimately read

this shit

All these philosophies

made me forget

that I have a lover

who just wants to hang out

in groups

What could be more unfortunate

for a cheapo,

a DESPO like me?

Yeah. I know I am called that

sometimes

just for wearing short skirts

that show off my long smooth legs

that other girls don't have

in the peak of winters

Neither do they have

dysfunctional families

friends who have no respect (for me)

a history of sin

for which there is no redemption

committed at an age

reserved for teddy bears when

I played with

a male's private parts

the ugly truth that little girls don't even get to see

leave alone touch and feel.

A past and perhaps

a poignant future of

learning difficulties

that made my mind wander

from a

trigonometric equation

to a word from the thesaurus I can replace 'sad'

with

to my father's stethoscope

to mama's tattoo on her navel

to *bhaiya's* muddy football

to the Barbie Uncle gave me

with her face now

damaged

eyes tired from always staying open

hair in disaster

and shabby old tight-fitting rags

She started looking so much like

I do

from the inside

You need to

love yourself Dolly

just look at you

who can match

these features?

this skin?

this figure?

this sense of style?

You are already a knockout

announced my mother

Oh cut the crap, Mama!

I have heard this a hundred times

as if it would

actually

make me

change my mind

Almost forty now

Mama

was holding on

to her youth

by spending all her time

in the gym

or next to the mirror

and she did a

bloody good job of it

We were more like friends

than mother and daughter

A friend . . .who knew nothing

about my dirty dark secrets

chiselled inside me

forever . . .

But my beauty

spread

far and wide

only Karan

still remained untouched

at least physically

But Mama

gave me the confidence

to carve

my own road

a road

that led

to the same lift

the same house

that Uncle brought me to

a hundred years ago

and now

I brought his son to

play

once again

Yes
this was meant to be
As his lips came near mine
I could smell the flavour of the same
refreshing peppermint
As his hands glided down
to my waist
I saw him

Standing at the door

with a wry smile

on his pale face

amused

dejected

in pain

for betraying him

Uncle!! I scream!!

Karan let go of me

What did you just say, Dolly?

Your father . . . I said, hushed . . .

I think he saw us...O shit man !!

My father, Dolly

lives

in Australia

Karan . . . I whispered again . . . he is back

go out and say hello

. . . Look, there is no one

relax, Dolly

maybe you are just nervous

Karan said

all creeped-out as he switched on the lights

of the main entrance

Mama, I swear I saw him

I mean someone

who looks like Uday Uncle

in the building . . .

is he back?

Well, if he is, I am not going to spare him

this time

for leaving just like that

Yeah, Mama, and now

he is back

just like that

You are so beautiful Dolly, so soft . . . red cheeks

I can never have enough

of you . . .

My body jerked in response

I woke up

startled

all wet

only now

it wasn't my pee down there

I need to see him

he is back

but why is he hiding?

Mama, did you find out?

Let's call him over for lunch

your best friend

Dolly, what the hell are you talking?

Uday isn't back

he called me last night

from Australia

said he was thinking about us

Us? You mean me, too? I thought

as a chill ran down my spine

I still need to see him

or

for now

his poor photocopy will do

Karan. The neighbourhood stud

girls swooned over him

guys wanted to be like him

Into music. Sports

And me

A complete package

yet

so incomplete

to me

God, just add those couple of decades

some more suave

and he might come close

to my illicit love

Starry, starry night

Paint your palette blue and grey . . .

For the first time

I felt a connection

with Karan

as we slow danced

to this tragedy of an artist's life . . .

Now I understand

What you tried to say to me

And how you suffered for your sanity . . .

I almost closed my eyes and felt

Karan's closeness

as if he

would rescue me

from the pain, the longing and the loathing

his father dug deep in my soul

Maybe

I should just give him a chance . . .

and not use him

to fulfil me

I open my eyes

as my body moves to the rhythm

next to his

slowly . . . softly . . .

and I see him . . .

Standing at the door

with the same wry smile

on his same pale face

amused

dejected

in pain

for betraying him

Uncle!! I scream!!

Karan, don't shit me

your dad's there, I saw him

he was looking at us

Dolly, stop playing these games

you don't want to get close

just say so

Karan is now on fire

and I melt

as he reminds me of the same heat

I felt around his dad's body

a long, long time ago

Yes . . . I was just fooling around, I apologise

and feel sorry

for myself

What's happening?

And who is really playing games?

Uncle is back

but no one wants to tell me

Does it mean

they know?

I am like the

pink handkerchief

tied

fluttering in the middle

between the two ends

of a game

of tug of war

pulled viciously

by the son and his father.

Whoever wins

or loses

forgets all about the

dangling piece of cloth

which is now

tossed aside.

With an imagination

as insane as mine

I started fearing

falling asleep

to ward off the random scenes

turning into full-fledged

lucid dreams

of both father and son

together

dissolving in the bed

with me

There came a point

when I wasn't sure

if I was awake

or sleeping

Only the fluorescent numbers

across my bed

confided in me

that there were hours to go

before the morning sun

came in through

to disinfect

my bed

with sweat trickling into

those creases

just like

the creases in my toxic mind

if only I wasn't too lazy

to smoothen them out

My friends

Tara and Megha

said they were worried about me

Tara took me to a workshop

in the society hall

where they teach

girls

how to say no

If only

I'd known

that I had a choice

I listened

and I broke down

I had to tell someone

even if it was nothing but lies

that Karan wanted

to go all the way

(but rather it was me…still we couldn't…because…his
father was always watching)

and it wasn't a lie

as they said I was telling

So he broke up with me

left me completely

on my own

to live out my fantasies

alone

Oh, how much I liked

him

I realised

only after he stopped

taking my calls

and called me

what I was:

M-A-D

Now I didn't know

what was true

and what wasn't

I saw his father

but he did not believe me

and said

I had issues

I had to sort out

and I had to stop flirting

as he was serious

about wanting a real relationship

not just physical intimacy

like me

I guess I was a bimbo

after all

I apologised

I couldn't

let him leave me

just like his father

Maybe if I met him around people

Uncle wouldn't mind

and I was right

Uncle stopped stalking us

so we continued

having our relationship

NOT being taken

to the next level

as I am sure

both my mama

and Uncle

would have disapproved

Here I was falling

in love now

floating in the clouds above

washed by and soaked in raindrops of true love

so clean

no kisses

no fondling

only pure

messages

of I love you baby

on Snapchat

Oh, how it felt

to be that precious girl

the chosen one

that girl who can have anyone

but wants no one except him

that girl who is finally falling in love slowly,
soberly, sweetly

with the handsome stud of the neighbourhood

who had eyes

only for her

Yes. Beautiful people

make love seem

even more pink

than pink teddy bears

We continued

our romance

despite

my record

with his father

I felt

we all could move on

and grow up

A couple of years more

till I was seventeen

and hated school

more and more until it was

just too much

so that

one day

I just quit

Part III

Coming of Age

You can't do that, Dolly!

my mama

laughed at my guts

that reminded her

of her younger self

I am not going there any more, Mama

I have nothing more to learn

than I already know

of which I can't remember

anything at all

What would your dad say?

Dr Aman Nanda's daughter

not even a high-school pass?

And it made her laugh even more

holding back

her tears of sorrow

for a failure of a daughter

of relief

for her daughter didn't have to suffer any more

of revenge

on her husband

whose blood

had let him down

big time

They were separated

but still some more tears remained

in anticipation

of the spiteful sarcasm

she

would be subjected from him

and the whole wide world

that she had failed too

in her most sacred duty

as a mother

But only she knew

she had given me enough courage

to make such a move

which in today's date and time

only the super-crazy or

the super-rich or the super-poor

can.

But here we were

the simpletons

the middle classes

maybe the upper-middle

or whatever

as if it mattered

The fact was

I was free

of the prison they called school

If only I could break free

from the prison of my mind

just like that, too!!

While my classmates slogged

cramming more and more formulas

I stayed at home

and tried to sleep

away the pain

of being called

slow, off, mental case

behind my back

sometimes on my face

while all I could do was

pretend

I did not hear their words

and did not understand

their sneers

that made them feel

good about themselves

simply because

a beautiful girl in their class

was so, so damn stupid

that she didn't stand a chance

of ever, ever

making it in life

and then they could forgive God

for making them ugly

At least they got marks

you know

Whoever invented the idea

that intelligent people

are those who know by heart

the names of

presidents and vice-presidents or
capitals or currencies

of the countries of the world

was the biggest dumb ass to begin with!

That's GK, dude!

So what next, asked Mama

I want to take it easy

Mama shrugged

as in her mind

her lazy spoiled daughter

already had it easy

till she remembered

a difficult childhood

of learning difficulties

and the struggles we had to go through

in order to stay

at a place

that didn't want me

a place

I had just rejected and didn't allow

any more

to squeeze me more and more

into an invisible bubble

a bubble I could not burst

but now could make it bigger so I could breathe

I had to stay inside, I guess

I had secrets to protect

and conspiracies

that made me

I had to stay inside, I guess
I had secrets to protect

But now that I was almost an adult

I knew

or had a divine revelation from the dark skies above

what happened to me

was not fair

Uncle

did not do it so Mama could live

I knew it then

and I laughed

at my sorry state

of pretending to myself

that I believed him

when I did it

because it… kinda felt nice

and now the agony I felt

because I had enough free time

to know

I was so so so so wrong!!

Why did Uncle and I

do this to me??

I was just a baby

how could he, God, how could he??

I screamed and screamed

silently

and my mind split open

created a mayhem of a million pieces

with blood, gore and acid oozing out fiercely

each piece felt a different feeling:

revulsion, hatred, disgust, remorse, paranoia

As I said, I am not so good with words

and anyway, those different feelings

mean the same shame

directed towards

the same thing

a dream

of him, his whole being slaughtered and sliced

into a million pieces too

I will get you one day

Uncle

I promised

to the little girl

There was only one problem

His son

had fallen deeply madly

in love

with a girl

who had snapped herself out of it

just like that

for a greater cause

a higher purpose

When I said I don't love you any more

as I have found someone else

I was almost right

but he didn't believe me

and begged me to stay

I had to break away

as I did not want collateral damage . . .

he

was too precious a boy

too loving and caring

a sweetheart

who had to be protected

from me

But his love for me

was perhaps

greater than my hate

for his father

so I gave up trying

to keep him out of this

Maybe I wasn't strong enough

to stand my ground

or maybe

I did love him

a fact that was coming

in the way

of my fantasises

of tormenting his father

more than he made me suffer now

for the pleasure I experienced then

A pleasure that took my mind off

from the torture of those times

of having a razor-sharp stone

between my legs

its hardness cutting through my insides

for which I made an excuse

bluffed like a pro

every time—

that I had a stomach-ache

that I got hit by a hard ball

that I tumbled down on something hard

in the playground

which weren't lies entirely

Mama believed me

maybe she didn't have the courage to take any more blows

or maybe believing was more convenient

After all everyone knew

I was the clumsy one,

in my own zone,

who hardly paid attention to the outside world

As a little girl
I had to wait

to cry

in my bed at night

with a monster underneath

I couldn't even

make much noise about it

It was as if it was

'a part of life'

like it's no big deal

But now that I was a grown-up—

Ok, you heard it before—

so, like I said, I was older

and wiser

had seen some documentaries

and some primetime news

and even read a book

I realised

I was just used

Abused

And I wondered why

my mama who is as modern, as liberal as it can get

never ever talked about this with me

The more I knew

the more I knew

that it was wrong

Uncle violated my trust

and my mama's

He had to pay for it

and this thought drove me insane

the obsession

to see him suffer

became a trending video

in my imagination

But with Karan

I was back again . . .

this on-off relationship

also became

'a part of life'

like it's no big deal

well…you know

it's complicated

In the life of a teenager

a three-four years relationship

with the same person

is a very serious business

like a lifetime

And even I

had begun to feel

committed

If only . . .

senior wasn't in the scene any more

and I could do something

to wipe off

every trace

of him

from this world

Valentine's day

is a good time

to take your relationship

to the next level,

something I used to insist

even when I was younger

But today

Karan did

and as usual

I did not

want to have a choice

It was dead quiet

except

our murmurs, our giggles

in his empty house

the same house

that brought back memories

Thank god

they had got a new floral sofa

and had painted the walls light yellow

So his lips

came close to mine

I closed my eyes

tight

to stop me from seeing

images from the past

and as his shivering hands

explored those angles and curves

I could feel

his presence again

Standing at the door

with the same wry smile

on his same pale face

amused

dejected

in pain

for betraying him

Uncle!! I scream

again

Karan, you dog!!

You are fucking with me again!

Don't tell me

he isn't back

Look, he is watching us!

I pointed towards Uncle

who stood

watching,

his eyes

piercing into mine

Karan! Look at him, your father! I shouted

Dolly! Stop it, you bitch . . .

no one's here

except you and me

Oh yes . . . oh yes . . . he is not there

so I am blind or a psycho?

Is that what you are saying?

You father and son!! In the whole goddamn world

was it only me

you both could find to mess around with??

As we turned back

Uncle

escaped

I fled too

to my mama

I cried

and cried

and cried

Sorry, Mama

I was making out with Karan

and Uncle saw us

My mama

who is as modern, as liberal as it can get

oh, I am repeating myself again

sorry

my mama

couldn't understand

why I was crying

and saying sorry

for being with my boyfriend

She knew about it and did not

really mind

so, what was the ruckus about?

Oh yes . . . Uncle saw us

Dolly, my baby

Uday isn't here

he hasn't visited India

since years

trust me *beta*

he called me from Australia just this morning

How about trusting me, Mama?

I blasted her

For once

when I am saying

he is here

he is here

He is just hiding

and why does he keep calling you?

Mama then realised

there was more to it

She begged me

to tell the truth

and when I refused stubbornly

despite hoping

that she would keep begging

she begged me again

to come with her

to see someone

she trusted

. . . I saw him three times

in Karan's house

I mean

it's his house . . . too

And what were you doing then? I mean anything in
particular or

common

to all these three times?

Yes . . . me and Karan . . . we were

sort of . . . close . . .

kissing and all . . . you know

The first two times . . . it was a couple of years back

and last time . . .

just last week . . .

Uncle is back . . .

I saw him . . . in flesh and bone

but they say I am lying

The doctor didn't want to talk any more she knew

there was so much more

and I wasn't ready

to let the monster out

My mother didn't ask me

any more questions

She just became sweeter

just like she was

when the first doctor revealed the naked truth

of my learning disabilities

ages ago

She was worried

there was something even murkier and savage

waiting to be exposed

though

she sort of had a very good idea by now

evidenced by the dark circles around her eyes

that she lay awake every night

praying

hoping

against hope

that her worst fears wouldn't come true

about her best friend

and her daughter

At my next appointment

we were ready

as it had weighed me down so much

and I was so injured

and so, so tired

that either I could fall flat on my face

with a thud

just like they show in movies

or

be my own hero

decide to stand up

with my fists closed

my teeth clenched

and blood finding its way out through

my combat uniform

a cross between Manikarnika and Bahubali

and to make it even more intense

say out aloud a motivational quote

a Sanskrit *shloka* would be perfect

Obviously, I didn't know any

so I made up my own:

'There is nothing that can get me'

But instead

I was cool

I let out

the steam

revealed those scars

and opened up

about how stupid I was

to allow this person

to control my very being

by playing a game

that shows no sign of ending

And that was quick!

Surprisingly

what I had lived and thought of

for thousands of hours

I summed up in just a few minutes.

as you know

I don't know

how to bullshit

and go on and on

to describe

my fucked-up stories

of pain and anguish and lust and deceit

It could have been so tragic, so shocking,

so sensational

if it had happened to a drama queen

who could throw tantrums

break some glasses

or play with complex words

unlike a Dumbo like

yours truly

Well . . . Mrs Nanda, said the doctor

I am afraid

she has got something.

It looks like . . .

well . . .

schizophrenia

combined with the usual anxiety issues . . .

She sees people

who are not there

she's delusional

or it's a hyperactive imagination . . .

to put it mildly

but it's a mental illness

we could try counselling

or medication . . . if needed

I am so sorry . . .

I need to run some more tests

to confirm

I am so sorry . . .

Here, have some water

Her treacherous past

her learning difficulties . . .

do you know

if this ADHD was acquired or was she born with it?

Maybe it's because of the abuse

we can't say for sure

it remains a grey area

but her current psychological issues

have manifested from

her episodes

with that predator . . .

a trusted one of the family, yes?

as usual

hmm . . .

I am so sorry, dear . . .

The doctor seemed heartbroken

What a nice lady, was all I thought

What a nice lady

said Mama too

on our way back

home

What were we supposed to do?

Mama did not

have a plan

She was tired

of Google already

and said she had done with reading for life . . .

so we decided

to give us some time

and let the grief

of the diagnosis

of the abuse

of the betrayal

sink in . . .

After all, what was the fuss?

Unlike then, which seemed like yesterday,

when I had to still get passing marks

to stay in school—

it was not like

Mama would throw me

out of the house, was it?

Would she?

I locked myself

in my room,

let the monster from

underneath the bed

come out

and laughed:

Hey, you don't have to hide any more

you can live with me

forever

Uncle Uday

on the other hand

disappeared

Karan broke up with me

one more time

maybe couldn't handle the situation

but this time

I needed him

more than ever

as Uncle came only

when Karan touched me

I had to see Uncle

one more time

Mama, look . . .

I have gone through shit

I am still not dead

Why are you behaving

as if

it's the end of the world?

It never is, my dear girl, it is never

the end of the world

It never is, my dear girl, it is never

Karan, please

I beg of you

will you make out with me

just this last time?

We can break up after that.

I need my answers

otherwise

I can

never move on

I did that

against

my doctor's advice

because

even my mama thought

that's the only way

we could move on

Yeah, my mama

was either very stupid herself

or believed in me just too much

for her own good

But still, my baby . . .

if you have to confront him

let's go and see him

in Australia . . . in person

or if you want to kill him

then let me do the honours

Mama fidgeted helplessly

with raging rivers of black molten lava

erupting from her furious eyes endlessly

Mama, I just need answers

from the man who stands watching

when I get touched by

another man

Karan, my precious one

gave in

when

he heard the whole damn saga

and why I wanted to be kissed by him

He has a good heart

unlike where he came from

a miserable place

You see, Dolly

my father, your Uncle Uday

left us, his family

one fine day and never came back

You don't know

how much I hate him

I have questions too

but I will let you

tackle him first

Karan, my precious one,

was sounding

crazier than even I was . . .

You see,

people

with troubled childhoods

never really grow up

and keep doing stupid things

With my mother's permission

I went again

to the same house

where his son was waiting for me

a boy, nervous

and yet

with a kindness

a strength of character, as the cliché goes,

that made me melt into his arms

despite my selfish intentions

to resolve my own issues

through this shadow

we both waited for

With streams of tears

running down to our mouths

we kissed and kissed

and tasted the salt

in each other

We knew

we were both in fact

applying balm

to each other's wounds

And sure enough

Standing at the door

with the same wry smile

on his same pale face

amused

dejected

in pain

for betraying him

Uncle!! I scream!!

yet again

Uncle . . . I turned towards him

and moved Karan's hands

from behind

over myself

guiding him

to places

Uncle had touched

my manic body now blazing

Don't stop, Karan . . . I ordered

I had to make sure

the father stayed

long enough

Me: Why are you back, Uncle?

Uncle: I cannot believe you would become a bad girl, Dolly

Me: Uncle, was I a bad girl when you had me?

Uncle: No, you were good

I loved you

and you loved me

and I thought

you will always love me

even if I left

I had given you

enough memories

to last a lifetime

Me: Uncle, do you know what you did was wrong?

Uncle: You were a part of it, Dolly

You wanted me, as I wanted you

Me: I was a little girl, Uday, you bastard

I was a little girl

You vomited your vulgarity all over me

made me impure for life

you robbed me

even when I had

nothing to give

your claws dug into my chest

that shuddered with pain

and took away my soul

burnt it mercilessly

then put the ashes back in . . .

And now, why are you back? Tell me what brings you back?

Uncle: I came back

to say sorry

will you forgive me?

for a sin committed for which no punishment is brutal enough

I was a demon with blood in my hands

I was a murderer of the spirit of an innocent child

but Dolly, never ever think it's your fault

forget what I said before

never think you are impure

because of what I did

you are pure . . . as pure as your mother's love

but will you forgive me, my dear little girl, my *kanjak*?

Me: Even if it's too much to ask for

I forgive you, Uncle

for I need to save myself

from my wrath

for I need my sanity

back, too

if I ever was sane

and when I know

I was never 'normal'

to begin with . . .

Uncle: So long, Dolly . . .

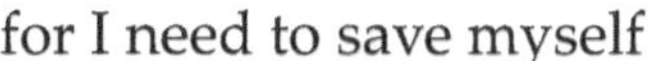

Uncle vanished

for good

It was all over

Or so I thought

Just then Mama walked in

her face

evaporated of all colour

What happened, Mama?

I asked

even though I had something

more important, more exciting to share

Karan, my child . . .

cried Mama

I just got a call from

Australia

Your dad's colleague . . .

he said your dad . . . met with an accident

. . . passed away last night . . .Uday, that son of a bitch!

Oh he will burn in hell!

 am so sorry

We all hugged and cried over our loss

Part IV
Closure

I regretted the impossibility

of seeing him suffer

and crying out in pain

and pleading at my feet

to forgive him

but I already did

I just needed to remind myself

again and again . . .

They say

- Stop telling yourself these negative stories about yourself

- You are God's creation, a miracle

- Be your best version

- Unburden yourself from your past

and blah blah blah.

But then, what's the rush again?

Why is a long long long

grieving,

a very very very

sad

period full of guilt and filth

not allowed?

Why couldn't I be left alone

to figure it out

myself?

I had started feeling secure in this place . . .

indulging myself in the soothing

comfort food

of self-pity

I also understood very well, I needed to get out

and waited for that time to come . . .

delaying it as much as I could . . .

I knew I couldn't jump-start the healing

but I had to start somewhere

I knew I couldn't jump-start the healing

It was now a year

that

he had left

And Karan, my precious one

the original hero

he had to leave too

for higher studies

promising

that he would come back for me

soon

I believed him

as I had started to believe in everything, too

He had his own demons to fight

and needed that space

While

I continued having trouble sleeping

and bouts of panic attacks here and there

But slowly . . .

from black

the sky started looking blue again

from yellow

the French fries golden

the Snapchat filters made me laugh again

I started missing my friends too

and it was time

to go back

to school

Knowledge is a powerful tool

let us not take it away

from kids

who have to acquire it

with difficulty

what you call learning difficulties

or disabilities

if at all it matters

The fact of the matter is that

kids like me

and all other kids too

just need respect

It was the last year in school

though when I left before

I had told everyone

I did it to become a model

As I was just confirming a stereotype

that beautiful girls = dumb = models

and of course

it validated them

and the gossip mongers created even more hype

But this time

even if it was kind of awkward to come back

I had to be honest

I needed to prove

that I wasn't finished

I was an interesting work-in-progress

And it did not mean

better percentages

it meant

more confidence

more positivity

more style than I already had, why not?

And

a resounding belief that no matter what

There is nothing that can get me

I know it's all *gyan*

but there has to be something good

that you can take away from

a sickening, wretched life like mine

so read more books

watch more movies

Bollywood best

play more sports

make your bed

talk to your mom

motivate that friend

mend some fences

don't judge

see a therapist if you have to

work through your problems

face your fears

dare

Be good.

Even if it's a paradox

And so, so unfair at times

this is the only shitty world we've got

so, if we can't fight it

we join in

Joining in can be fun sometimes

And who says we can't still change the world?

Of course we can

That's why we are here

People close to you can be weirdos

but they are your own people, your own friends, your own family

even when rebelling is a young person's second nature

sometimes

you sit back

and believe

and sure enough

everything will be alright

Maybe I haven't been able to give you your

Happy Ending

but I continue breathing . . .

and just as the proof of the pudding is in the eating

the purpose of life is in the living

Mere jaisa koi hard'ich nahi hai

—from the movie *Gully Boy*

Dear Reader,

This is the third and final part of my Teen Book Series.

The books tell the coming-of-age stories of three friends—Tara in *Sick of Being Healthy*, Megha in *Dying to Live* and, finally, Dolly in *Dolly Won't Play*.

These are motivational, entertaining, contemporary novels with pictures, raising some serious issues that teens face, such as low self-esteem, academic pressures, complicated online relationships and psychological problems, in a light-hearted way. Well . . . maybe not this one. But you get the gist.

Sick of Being Healthy and *Dying to Live* have received rave reviews and been on the bestselling list of their categories and part of 'Memorable Books' on Amazon. Though all books stand on their own and can be read separately, for a better experience it might make more sense if read in a sequence. The choice is entirely yours.

Love and light,

Monisha K Gumber